This edition published by Parragon Books Ltd in 2015

Parragon Books Ltd
Chartist House
15–17 Trim Street
Bath BA1 1HA, UK
www.parragon.com

ISBN 978-1-4748-1397-6

Printed in China

A Splashing Date

Bath · New York · Cologne · Melbourne · Delhi
Hong Kong · Shenzhen · Singapore · Amsterdam

One lovely summer's day, Mickey Mouse asked his girlfriend, Minnie, if she'd like to go for a boat ride.

"I would love to," Minnie said with a smile.
"A nice, easy float on the lake sounds like the perfect way to spend the day."

    Mickey and Minnie
were preparing to set sail when
Goofy came running by.

    "Hiya, Mickey. Hiya, Minnie," he said and waved.
"What a great day for a boat ride!"

    Goofy was looking at Mickey's boat and didn't see
a squirrel crossing his path. He accidentally stepped
on its tail.

The squirrel leaped away and landed in the boat.

Mickey and Minnie were so startled that they jumped up, making the boat rock.

Mickey tried to stop the rocking, but he couldn't. The boat tipped over, sending Mickey and Minnie into the water!

Luckily, Donald
Duck was nearby in his
speedboat and saw what
had happened.

He helped Mickey and Minnie into his boat. "Why don't you ride with me for a while?" he said. "You can relax, take it easy and let the engine do the work."

Mickey and Minnie sat back and relaxed. They had just reached the middle of the lake when the boat's engine suddenly stopped.

"Oh, no! What do we do now?" Minnie asked.

"I have an idea," Donald said. He took off his hat and started to paddle with it.

Mickey and Minnie did the same. Huffing and puffing, they made their way back to shore.

"How about some lunch while we dry off?" Mickey said.

Minnie agreed and the two were soon relaxing in the Sun with hot dogs.

As they were enjoying their lunch, Pluto came running past. When he saw the delicious hot dogs, he decided he wanted one, too. He jumped into Mickey's lap and tried to grab the food!

"Stop it, boy!" cried Mickey.

"Pluto," said Minnie, "if you want a hot dog, we can get you one."

But it was too late. Pluto knocked Mickey and Minnie right into the water!

Poor Mickey and Minnie climbed out of the
lake and settled on the grass to dry off again.
Soon, Donald Duck's nephews, Huey, Dewey
and Louie, came by in their sailing boat.

"Hey, Mickey," called Dewey. "Would you and
Minnie like to borrow our boat to go sailing? There's
a good wind today."

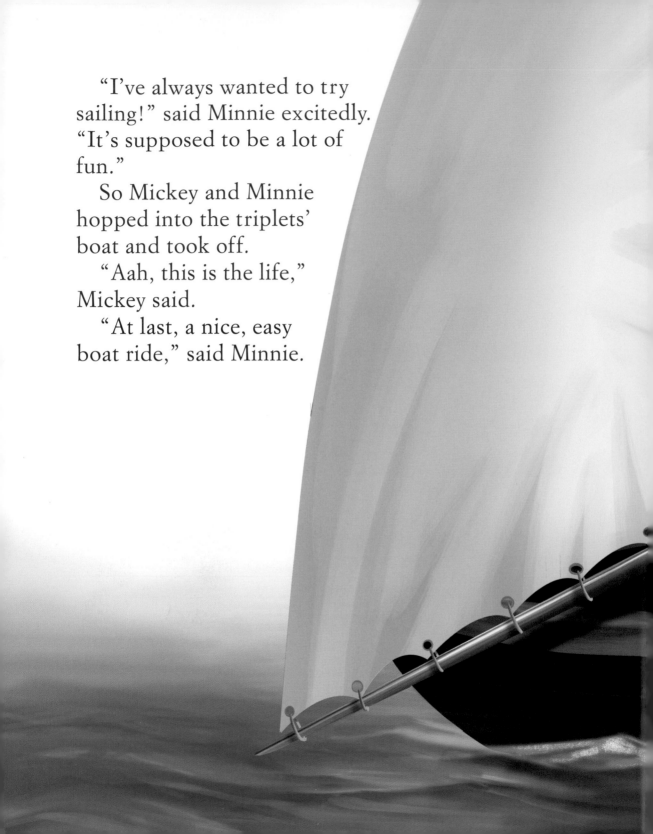

"I've always wanted to try sailing!" said Minnie excitedly. "It's supposed to be a lot of fun."

So Mickey and Minnie hopped into the triplets' boat and took off.

"Aah, this is the life," Mickey said.

"At last, a nice, easy boat ride," said Minnie.

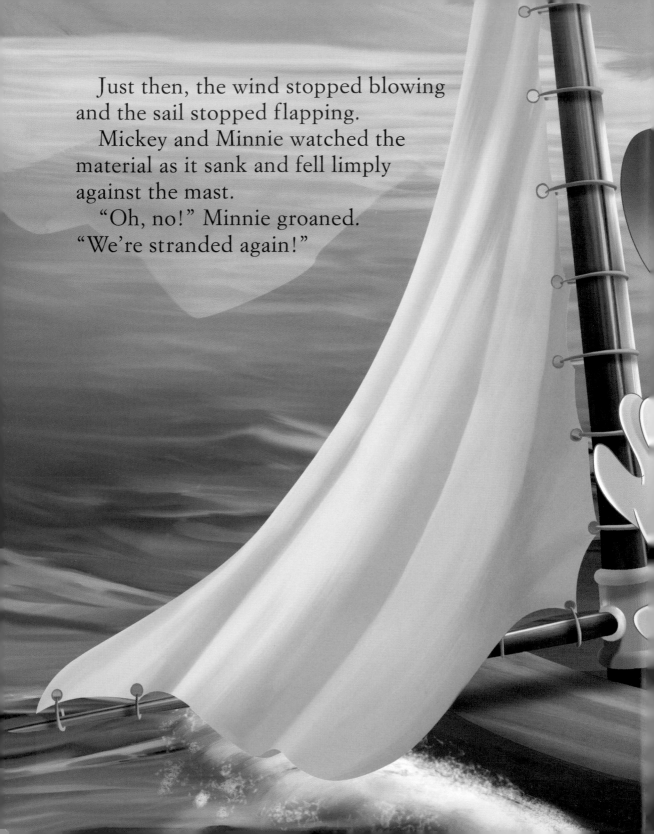

Just then, the wind stopped blowing and the sail stopped flapping.

Mickey and Minnie watched the material as it sank and fell limply against the mast.

"Oh, no!" Minnie groaned. "We're stranded again!"

Mickey and Minnie tried to paddle with their hands, but it was no use. They kept going round in circles.

Suddenly, Mickey looked up.

Goofy and Donald
were coming towards
them in rowing boats.
"We thought you
might need some help,"
said Donald. He and Goofy
attached a rope to the sailing boat and
towed Mickey and Minnie across the lake.
The happy couple didn't have to do
a thing!

As the Sun began to set over the peaceful lake, Mickey and Minnie sat back and relaxed. They had *finally* managed to have a nice, easy boat ride!